This book belongs to:

_____

_____

Gemma

Lennon

Fairy stories

FOR BEDTIME

Illustrated by
JANE LAUNCHBURY

HUTCHINSON

LONDON · MELBOURNE · AUCKLAND · JOHANNESBURG

Produced by Templar Publishing Ltd,
107 High Street, Dorking, Surrey, RH4 1QA,
for Hutchinson Children's Books

Text copyright © Templar Publishing 1987
Illustrations copyright © Templar Publishing 1987

First published 1987 by Hutchinson Children's Books
An imprint of Century Hutchinson Ltd
Brookmount House, 62-65 Chandos Place, Covent Garden,
London WC2N 4NW

Century Hutchinson Group (Australia) Pty Ltd,
16-22 Church Street, Hawthorn, Melbourne, Victoria 3122

Century Hutchinson Group (NZ) Ltd,
32-34 View Road, PO Box 40-086, Glenfield, Auckland 10

Century Hutchinson Group (SA) Pty Ltd,
PO Box 337, Bergvlei 2012, South Africa

Set in Melior Roman by Templar Type

Colour separations by Positive Colour Ltd, Maldon, Essex
Printed and bound by
L.E.G.O., Vicenza, Italy

British Library Cataloguing in Publication Data

Fairy stories for bedtime.
I. Launchbury, Jane
823'.01'089282 [J]   PZ7

ISBN 0-09-173472-X

CONTENTS

THE
FAIRY
POSTBOX

by Philip Steele

Jimmy Jones was a postman, and he drove a little red van. Every day he went from one postbox to the next. He opened each box, collected up the letters from inside and stuffed them into his big, brown sack. Now, the very last postbox on Jimmy's round was at the end of a long and lonely lane. It was built in an old brick wall at the edge of the Wild Wood. Ivy and bindweed crept all around it, and brambles hung down, showering it with their blossoms in the spring.

"I don't know why I bother," Jimmy would grumble every afternoon as he drove down the lonely lane. "Nobody posts any letters here any more." He would then look up at the trees of the wood and shiver. "This place gives me the creeps!" he would mutter, and speed back to town in his van.

Jimmy didn't realise that the postbox at Wild Wood was over a hundred years old. When it had first been built, the lane was very busy. Every day the box had been filled to the brim with letters to the town and to faraway places, with Christmas cards and birthday cards and bills and picture postcards. But then the big road had been built. Nobody strolled down the lane any more. Nobody walked through Wild Wood, and the postbox was soon forgotten.

Now one very cold winter, it snowed and snowed for days on end. Huge white drifts blanketed the lane. Jimmy Jones stayed by the fire in the post office, and did not visit the lonely old postbox. But for the first time in years, other people did ... in the still small hours of the morning. They were tiny folk about the size of your little finger, and they flitted in and out of Wild Wood on wings of shimmering blue. If you had seen them, you would have thought that it was just a flurry of snow in the wind. If you had heard them, you might have thought it was just the babbling of a distant brook.

And what do you think they were saying to each other? Well, fairies are not so different from the rest of us. They may be just a little bit smaller than us, but they still talk about the weather!

"This north wind will be the end of me!" grumbled Elidir, as he slid down an icicle. Arabella nodded and fluttered her wings to keep warm.

"Wild Wood in the winter is no fit place for fairy folk. We need a nice home like humans have. With a roof over our heads, we'd be as warm as toast!" she said.

"As snug, as snug could be!" agreed Crystal dreamily.

It was then that Elidir noticed the old postbox. He tiptoed over a bank of glistening snow, and then flew up to the slit in the front where the letters go. At last he dared to take a peek inside. It was warm and cosy in there!

"Come on in!" he piped to the others. "Come and see our new home!"

A few days later, Jimmy Jones was at the post office in the town. He was enjoying a cup of tea with Mrs Cratchitt, the post-mistress.

"The snow's still too bad for me to go out," he was saying. "Wild Wood has been cut off for days."

Mrs Cratchitt shook her head. "It's hardly worth going out there, is it Jimmy? Nobody uses that box any more. Why don't we seal it up and forget all about it?"

"As far as I'm concerned, you can knock down the whole wall," said Jimmy, as he sipped the tea from his saucer. "Wild Wood's a waste of time."

Now as it happened, one of the fairies from Wild Wood had flown into town that very afternoon. Crystal was on tooth-fairy duty that week. She was going from

house to house collecting children's teeth, and leaving coins under their pillows in return. As Crystal fluttered past the post office, she couldn't help but hear what Mrs Cratchitt was saying to Jimmy Jones.

They were going to take away the postbox where she had made her nice new home! As Crystal flew back over the snowdrifts, tears froze on her cheeks. She slipped back into the old red box in the wall, and told the others what was going on. "Something must be done!" said Arabella. "We must save our new home!" And they put their heads together to think of a suitable plan.

After a fortnight, the snow began to melt. The ditches filled with water. Jimmy Jones was able to drive his van out of the town once again. He drove down to Wild Wood, whistling as he went.

"Well, I won't be coming out here much longer," he said to himself. "When we seal up the old box, I'll be home half an hour earlier!"

Jimmy parked the van and walked over to the postbox. He had a strange feeling he was being watched. What a weird place this was! Jimmy put his key in the box and opened the little door. The box was full of letters! Jimmy could hardly believe his eyes. There were envelopes of every shape and size! Jimmy sorted through them. They were all stamped and addressed correctly, but some of the names on the envelopes were a little strange, to say the least... 'Queen Erica of the Hollow Hills' ... 'Chief Dwarf of the Black Forest' ... 'To Mirabelle from Stardust'...

Every day it was the same. Jimmy Jones filled his sack with letters from Wild Wood.

"I'm sorry, Jimmy," said Mrs Cratchitt one day. "We just can't get rid of the Wild Wood postbox now. It's the busiest one on the whole of your round."

Elidir, Crystal, Arabella and the other fairies were delighted. They had a home for all seasons. When the summer sun made the lane hot and dusty, they could sleep in the cool shade of the postbox. And when autumn winds sent leaves scurrying down from Wild Wood, they could snuggle down among the letters, away from the damp and draughts.

The fairies even introduced themselves to Jimmy Jones, and they became quite friendly. He didn't tell Mrs Cratchitt, though, in case she laughed at him. These days, not many people believe in fairies. Do you?

Next time you go to post a letter, put your ear to the box. Can you hear anything? Are you sure there's not a scampering sound inside? Or the echo of tinkling laughter? Or is it just the wind blowing through the branches of the trees, and the patter of raindrops on the pavement?

THE END

NOEL THE KNOW-ALL GNOME

by Jane Launchbury

Underneath the Christmas tree sat a very odd shaped present. When her husband wasn't looking, Mrs Jones squeezed it, shook it, poked it, and looked at it from all angles, but she couldn't work out what it could possibly be. It was obviously going to be a lovely surprise.

On Christmas morning, Mr Jones picked up the present and gave it to his wife.

"This is for you, darling," he said with a big smile. "I hope you like it."

Mrs Jones took a deep breath and started to tear off the wrapping paper. A bright red shiny hat appeared, with bright yellow spots. Underneath the hat was a bright pink face with a shiny red nose. Mrs Jones gave a gasp as she pulled off the rest of the wrapping paper, for

it revealed the most ghastly garden gnome
she had ever seen! The colours were so
bright that she thought they would
probably glow in the dark.

"I just knew you'd love him,"
said Mr Jones happily. "He's an
Extra-Special-de-Luxe Limited
Edition Gnome," he added,
"of very superior quality.
I thought we could
call him Noel, seeing
that it's Christmas."

"What a good idea," muttered Mrs Jones picking up
the gnome by his big shiny nose and rushing for the back
door. "I can't wait to put him out in the garden."

She hurried down the garden path wondering
wherever her husband could have found quite such a
dreadful creature. She had never liked garden gnomes,
and this one seemed a particularly awful specimen. He
was so unbelievably bright and shiny, and he had a
very snooty smile. Mrs Jones resisted the temptation to
throw the gnome into the pond. She plonked him down
behind a bush instead, and hoped she wouldn't be able
to see him from the house. But Noel's colours were so
bright that he stood out from the rest of the garden like a
sore thumb.

When she had disappeared inside, Noel the gnome stretched his legs and peered down his nose at his new surroundings. He didn't like what he saw. This was no place for a gnome of his superior quality – it was far too dull and dreary. All those boring browns and greens would have to go for a start, and he immediately began planning how he would set about changing things for the better.

If Mrs Jones didn't like the new gnome, the real gnomes and fairies that lived in the garden weren't too pleased either. They had never seen anything quite like Noel before and, as soon as they were sure that there was no one about, they crept out of the trees and bushes to have a closer look. Noel didn't see them coming, of course, because real gnomes and fairies blend in so well with their surroundings that they are almost invisible.

Noel was bending down polishing his shiny shoes until he could see his bright pink face in them, when he realised that there were other faces reflected in them too. He looked up, and for the first time he noticed the gnomes and fairies around him. He sniffed and peered down his nose at the soft grey and brown creatures. They looked to him as though they could all do with a good wash and, being a superior sort of gnome who believed in speaking his mind, he told them so. Then just for good measure, he added that he thought everything in the garden needed a good wash and a few coats of colour, and he was going to have to do something about it. Then he realised that he still hadn't introduced himself.

"My name is Noel, and I'm an Extra-Special-de-Luxe Limited Edition Gnome," he announced grandly.

"Know-all?" said one of the fairies thoughtfully. "That's a very unusual name."

It didn't take long for the fairies and gnomes to decide that "Know-all" was in fact a very good name for the new gnome. He seemed to think he knew everything, and he had a way of looking down his big red nose at everyone that made them feel very uncomfortable. But they were kind creatures so they all decided to try and make him feel at home.

Then one day, Noel pushed his luck a bit too far. He got up very early in the morning, mixed up gallons of brightly coloured paints and set about "improving" the colour scheme in the garden. By the time the other gnomes and fairies realised what he was doing, he had painted all the tree trunks bright orange with turquoise spots, and was cheerfully painting the lawn pink with purple stripes!

The fairies and gnomes were horrified. And they all had to work very hard to put things back to normal before Mr and Mrs Jones woke up! They decided that something had to be done about Noel. But what?

In the end, it was Mrs Jones who dealt with the situation. She had been getting more and more fed up with seeing Noel glowing among the bushes, and on this particular morning he seemed brighter than ever.

"I hate that ugly gnome, he's a real eyesore," she grumbled as she put out some bread for the birds. She knew she couldn't throw him in the dustbin, but she didn't see any harm in temporarily "losing" him. So she looked around the garden for somewhere to hide him, and noticed the compost heap. That would do nicely... She took a big spade and dug a deep hole right in the middle. Then she picked up Noel, dropped him into the hole, and piled the compost back on top of him. The fairies and gnomes couldn't believe their luck.

But the strange thing was that life simply wasn't the same without Noel around. Although he had been an eyesore, and a bossy know-all, most of the fairies and gnomes had to admit that they had admired his enthusiasm and energy. It was just the way he went about things that was all wrong. Even Mrs Jones felt there was something missing from the garden, though she couldn't put her finger on what it was.

At first Noel had been absolutely furious about being buried in the compost heap, but there was nothing he could do about it. Then he started to feel sorry for himself. Deep under the compost, he began to wonder what it was he had done wrong. Perhaps being an Extra-Special-de-Luxe Limited Edition Gnome wasn't quite so wonderful after all. He only knew he was superior because Mr Jones had said so, and what if Mr Jones was wrong? He certainly didn't look like any of the other gnomes. And then there was the matter of the "improvements". Even he had to admit that the garden had looked a bit odd after he tried changing the colour scheme. He was still wondering about this when he heard the sound of digging above him.

Some of the fairies and gnomes had felt so sorry for Noel that they had decided to rescue him. They very nearly missed him, for instead of the bright colours they had been expecting, Noel was coated from head to foot in sticky brown compost.

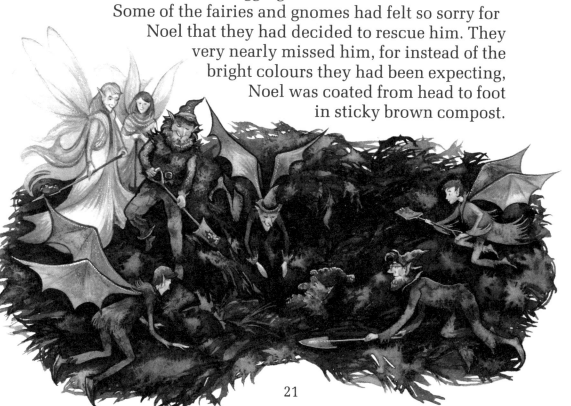

"You look as though you need a good wash!"
observed a tall brown gnome. And for once Noel had the
sense to say not a word. He was carried over to the
pond, where they set about scrubbing the compost off
with tiny scrubbing brushes. At first no one noticed
what was happening. Then they realised that not only
was the compost coming off, but so too were those
dreadful bright colours. Underneath, Noel was a lovely

shade of sandy brown. They scrubbed away until all the
colours had come off and Noel looked just like an
ordinary gnome. He stared at his reflection, and had to
admit that it was a distinct improvement. He even heard
several fairies comment about his good looks.

No one ever did work out quite what had happened
to Noel in the compost heap, but he was a changed

character afterwards. Instead of telling everyone what to do, he asked their advice. And when spring came, he learned to love the colours of nature (though he always liked the brighter ones best of all), and he turned out to be a very good gardener.

As for the Joneses, they had the most glorious garden in the village. Mr Jones always said jokingly that it must have been because of Noel, though he had been most upset about the way all his colours had washed off in the rain. Mrs Jones just smiled. She never did work out how he had got out of the compost heap, nor how he had lost his snooty smile and gained a very endearing twinkle in his brown eyes...

THE END

THE
WISHING
FAIRY

by Andrew Matthews

Sarah and Violet were twins, but they were not at all alike.

Sarah had fair hair and was a kindly girl. While her father and mother were out working on the farm where they lived, Sarah swept the floors and washed the dishes. Violet, on the other hand, had dark hair and was a selfish, vain girl. She was supposed to help with the housework, but instead she stayed in her bedroom, combing her hair and dreaming of the day when a rich and handsome gentleman would carry her off to be his wife. But Sarah was so good-hearted that she never told tales about her lazy sister.

Then one Saturday morning, Mother called Sarah and Violet up to her bedroom. Mother's eyes were watering and her nose was red.

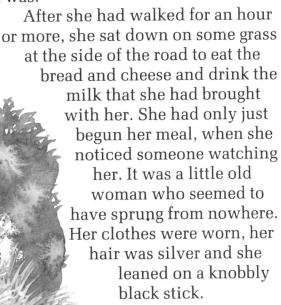

"I've got the most awful cold," she explained. "So I can't take the basket of eggs to market today. You two girls must do it for me."

Now, Violet didn't like this idea at all.

"Ah-choo!" she sneezed. "I think I've caught a cold as well! I must go straight back to bed. Sarah can bring me some warm milk before she leaves for market!" And although Sarah knew her sister was just pretending, she did just that before setting off down the road to town.

It was a hot day. The road was dry and dusty and the basket of eggs made Sarah's arms ache. But instead of complaining to herself, she breathed in the fresh air and listened to the birds singing in the trees and thought what a lovely day it was.

After she had walked for an hour or more, she sat down on some grass at the side of the road to eat the bread and cheese and drink the milk that she had brought with her. She had only just begun her meal, when she noticed someone watching her. It was a little old woman who seemed to have sprung from nowhere. Her clothes were worn, her hair was silver and she leaned on a knobbly black stick.

25

"My!" cried the old lady. "What a hot day it is, and how tired and hungry and thirsty I am!"

Sarah instantly felt sorry for the old woman.

"Sit next to me grandmother," she said politely. "You can rest on the soft grass and share my food and drink if you like."

"What a kind girl you are!" exclaimed the old woman, and she sat down as Sarah had suggested. When she had finished eating and drinking, the old woman winked at Sarah.

"What would you say if I told you that I was a fairy?" she asked. Sarah thought for a moment.

"I would believe you grandmother, for you have such a kind face," she replied.

"Prettily answered!" chuckled the old lady. "And you would be right to do so, for I am the Wishing Fairy! Now, take my stick and tap it on the ground three times, then see what happens."

Sarah did as she was told and tapped the stick on the ground. One! Two! Three! All at once, the eggs flew out of the basket and broke in half on the ground. But instead of the usual yellow yolk, out poured all sorts of wonderful things. Ruby rings, silver combs, silk scarves and a leather purse full of gold coins lay on the road.

"These things are all yours," said the Wishing Fairy. "They are a reward for your kindness and I hope they bring you happiness."

Overjoyed, Sarah gathered up the treasures and ran home.

Her mother and father were amazed when they heard all about Sarah's adventure. Violet was terribly jealous.

"Little Miss Goody-Goody!" she muttered to herself. "I bet I can do better than her." And, forgetting she was supposed to have a cold, she put some eggs in a basket, along with some good things to eat and drink, and set off down the road to town.

It was still a hot day, and before long Violet longed to sit down.

"I will not stop until I see the old woman," she said to herself, and forced herself to walk on. But she hadn't gone much farther before she was saying, "Bother the silly old nuisance! Why doesn't she appear? I'm sure Sarah didn't have to walk this far!" And not long after that she said, "I can't go on. This is really too unfair. I must sit down and have something to eat and drink!"

So she sat down at the side of the road and unpacked the hamper of food she had brought with her. Out came ham and cold chicken, fresh bread, cream cakes and some cool milk to drink.

Before she had time to eat anything, Violet noticed a young girl watching her from the other side of the road. She was dressed in rags and was leaning on a knobbly old stick.

"What do you want?" said Violet rudely, carefully unwrapping some juicy tomatoes.

"My!" cried the child. "What a hot day it is and how tired and hungry and thirsty I am!"

"Serves you right!" said Violet, stuffing a piece of chicken into her mouth. "You should have packed something to bring with you as I did."

"I see," said the girl. "And what would you say if I told you that I was the Wishing Fairy that your sister met this morning?"

Now, Violet was quite taken aback by this, but she soon recovered her senses.

"My sister told me all about you," she said. "So give me that stick at once! I want some silk scarves too, and emerald rings instead of ruby ones, and gold combs instead of silver!"

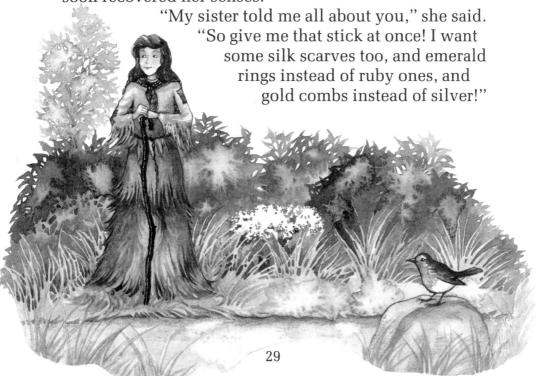

29

So saying, she grabbed the stick and banged it three times upon the ground. The eggs in her basket flew into the air. But instead of breaking on the ground to reveal the beautiful treasures Violet expected, they smashed over her head, covering her from head to foot in slimy, smelly egg yolk. When she looked up, there before her stood the old woman, leaning on her stick and chuckling merrily.

"I want my reward!" wailed Violet.

"You've got just what you deserved, my girl!" laughed the old woman. "Let this be a lesson to you." And with that, the stick flew up into the air and began to whack Violet hard. She ran home as fast as she could, with the stick chasing her all the way. But when she got to the front gate, it vanished into thin air with a whoosh.

After that, Violet mended her ways. She helped Sarah with the housework and stopped being so lazy and horrid. In the end, her dream came true – she did marry a rich, handsome gentleman. And so did Sarah. But those are two different stories...

THE END

FLORENCE AND WILFRED

by Sally Sheringham

Florence was an elderly fairy. She lived in a snug little cottage with her best friend, a marmalade cat called Wilfred. Florence was very happy on the whole, except every now and then she longed to be young and beautiful again.

"But I like you just the way you are," Wilfred would say, and Florence would reply that a cat – and a *male* cat, at that – couldn't possibly understand how she felt.

For Florence's 195th birthday, Wilfred gave her a pair of warm, sensible slippers.

"It's very kind of you, Wilfred dear," sighed Florence, "but these slippers make me feel even older." Then Florence suddenly had a brilliant idea. "I know!" she exclaimed. "I'll give myself a birthday present – I'll use my magic to become young and beautiful again.

Don't you think that's a brilliant idea Wilfred?"

"Humph," said Wilfred. "I think it's a very unbrilliant idea if you ask me." And he stalked off with his nose in the air.

The 'Young and Beautiful' spell turned out to be very complicated and Florence missed having Wilfred to help her. She had to find unpleasant ingredients like slugs, bugs and other slimy things too nasty to mention.

At last everything was assembled in a saucepan. She waved her magic wand. There was a bright blue flash and the concoction started to boil and smoke.

When it cooled down she poured the potion into a silver goblet and drank it. It tasted as revolting as it looked.

"I suppose even fairies have to suffer to be beautiful," Florence sighed, pulling a face.

Then she went upstairs, stood in front of the mirror and waited. She felt rather nervous...

Suddenly the magic started! FIZZ! Her straight white hair turned jet black and started to curl. WHIZZ! Her wrinkled cheeks and crumpled wings turned as smooth as if they'd just been ironed. ZIZZ! Her plump, cuddly body turned sleek and curvy.

Wilfred, who had heard all the fizzing and whizzing from the garden, watched disapprovingly from the doorway.

"Just look at me," Florence gasped. "I must be the most beautiful fairy in the world. Er – you don't think I've overdone the spell a bit, do you Wilfred?"

"A *bit*?" growled Wilfred. "That's putting it mildly. It's bound to lead to trouble if you ask me." But Florence just ignored him.

"I feel pretty – oh so pretty," she sang, twirling round and round in a cornflower blue dress she hadn't been able to fit into since she was eighteen.

33

"Humph," said Wilfred. "Personally, I preferred you the way you were." But Florence just told him not to be such a spoilsport.

During her birthday tea, Florence kept rushing off to the mirror to admire herself. She hardly ate any of the pink cake Wilfred had baked for her.

"It's delicious, Wilfred dear, but I don't want to spoil my new slim figure," she said, tossing her black curls.

"Humph," said Wilfred again.

But there was one thing Florence had overlooked in her desire to be young and beautiful – and that was that all the goblins and elves and gnomes for miles around would fall in love with her. It wasn't long before they were queuing at her door! In just one week she received ten boxes of chocolates, nine bunches of flowers, eight gold rings and seven offers of marriage.

Soon Florence spent all her time being wooed by doting admirers and having sweet nothings whispered in her ear.

"I might as well be a bit of furniture for the amount of interest she's showing in me," Wilfred thought sulkily as he sat alone by the fire.

The weeks went by and after a while Florence grew tired of being chased by all the gnomes, goblins and elves. She couldn't even go shopping without would-be husbands pursuing her, and the sweet nothings were getting extremely boring. Then one night she had a horrible dream about being married to a particularly ugly elf and, when she woke up, it suddenly struck her that Wilfred was better company than all her admirers put together.

The next morning Florence and Wilfred were enjoying a quiet breakfast together when, all of a sudden, a fat gnome started to recite love poems through the window. If that wasn't bad enough, a bald goblin with a box of chocolates started to bang on the door, and a lanky elf tried to climb down the chimney with a bunch of red roses.

"Oh, Wilfred, we can't even have breakfast in peace any more," cried Florence sadly. "My nerves won't stand it. Please send them away before I go mad."

Wilfred rose to his full height. The marmalade hairs on his back stood on end and his whiskers bristled.

"My mistress won't be receiving visitors today, or tomorrow, or ever again," Wilfred announced in his most important voice. "So may I bid you gentlemen good-day?"

Wilfred could look quite fierce when he wanted to; he certainly did then, and Florence's suitors hurried off. "I have to admit that being young and beautiful has a few disadvantages," said Florence with a sigh. "Would you mind helping me change back into my old self, Wilfred dear?"

"It would be a pleasure," said Wilfred.

Together they prepared the magic potion. This time, it tasted even more revolting! Then – FIZZ! Florence's curly black hair turned straight and white. WHIZZ! Her wrinkles returned. ZIZZ! Her body became lumpy and cuddly again.

Her suitors were all very puzzled. Whatever had happened to the young, beautiful fairy?

"She's gone away – for good," Wilfred told them firmly.

That evening, Florence and Wilfred sat cosily by the fire playing Snap. Florence wore her birthday slippers and munched a cream doughnut because she no longer had to worry about her figure. Wilfred was purring.

"I've just decided, Wilfred dear, that I really rather like being old and ugly," said Florence. "It's so much more restful."

"And the company's better," said Wilfred dryly. "Snap!"

THE END

THE ELF BULL

by Andrew Matthews

Farmer Hardacre charged into the kitchen panting and puffing and all of a dither.

"You'll never guess what I've found, Meg!" he told his astonished wife. "No, not if you guess for the next hundred years!"

"I shan't waste my time trying then!" snapped Mrs Hardacre. "You'd best tell me and have done with it." Without more ado, Farmer Hardacre slipped his knapsack off his shoulder, placed it on the kitchen table and opened it.

Inside the knapsack was a tiny bull, no bigger than a kitten. Its coat was black and glossy, its horns and hooves shone like silver, and its eyes glowed as red as two splinters of ruby. A fine gold chain was fastened around its neck like a collar.

"I found it caught in the thorn hedge down the lane," explained Farmer Hardacre. "I couldn't believe my eyes.

Did you ever see the like in all your born days?"

Mrs Hardacre went quite pale.

"Jack!" she whispered. "You take that creature back where you found it this very minute."

"But, Meg..."

"No buts, Jack!" insisted Mrs Hardacre. "That be an Elf Bull and Elf Bulls belong to the Elves!"

"'Tis mine," said the farmer stubbornly. "I found it! And I mean to take this fine little chap to market right away. I reckon some fancy lord or lady would pay a pretty penny for a poppet like this! Put on your finest dress, Meg, for we're off to town."

"Not me!" said Mrs Hardacre, shaking her head. "I'll have no part of such foolishness! Elves be tricky little things. No good will come of it, Jack, you mark my words!" But Farmer Hardacre chose to ignore his wife's warning. He bustled off to the stable, hitched up the pony and trap and set off on the road to town.

Before long, he met a strange little man perching on a milestone at the side of the road. His boots, breeches and jerkin were bright green, his face was nut-brown and his eyes twinkled merrily. But the strangest thing about him was his ears – for they were long and pointed.

"Oh-ho!" thought Farmer Hardacre as he reined his pony to a halt, for he knew an Elf when he saw one.

"Good day, Farmer Hardacre!" said the little man.

"Good day, Master Elf! And what can I do for you?" replied Farmer Hardacre in his most polite voice.

"You've got something that belongs to me in that old knapsack of yours," said the Elf.

"What's mine is mine!" returned the farmer rudely. "Finders keepers!"

But instead of getting cross, the Elf smiled.

"If you be a friend to the Elves, they'll be friends to you," he said. "But if you steal what belongs to them, woe betide you!"

"Hah!" scoffed the farmer even more rudely. "I'm off to market to do business, and talking to you is just a waste of time! Do your worst, little green fellow!" So saying, the farmer grasped the reins of his pony and continued on his way.

"It won't be as easy as you think...," he heard the Elf call after him, but he shrugged off the words and set his mind back to thinking of a purse fat with gold coins. After all, what could the Elves possibly do to a big strong farmer like him.

41

Town was busy and it took Farmer Hardacre a long time to find the spot he wanted. It was right in the middle of the town square, next to the horse-trough. He hitched up his pony, then stood up in the trap and started shouting to attract attention.

"Roll up, roll up! Come and take the chance of a lifetime!" he cried. "Have your money ready! Feast your eyes on an amazing sight!"

Farmer Hardacre bawled so loudly that before long a large crowd had gathered around him.

"What I've got for sale is one of the wonders of the world!" announced the farmer. "You'll see something that'll make your eyes pop out. In years to come you'll tell your grandchildren about what I'm carrying in my knapsack!"

"Show us then!" called someone in the crowd. Farmer Hardacre held up his hand for silence.

"You must prepare yourselves," he warned, "for no-one here will have seen the like before, no, nor ever will again, I daresay!"

42

So saying, he placed his hand in the knapsack, closed his fingers around what he felt inside and drew it out for all to see.

"There now!" he cried. "Seeing is believing!" But to his dismay, instead of the astonished gasps he had expected, the crowd burst into peals of laughter. The farmer glanced at his hand and saw, not the Elf Bull, but a string of pork sausages. So the Elves had got their own back after all.

"Swindled by magic!" he cursed. Farmer Hardacre became so angry, that the crowd, laughing, threw him in the horse-trough to cool him down.

The farmer drove home a sadder, wiser and wetter man. When he reached the milestone, he found the Elf still waiting.

"I told you it wouldn't be easy, Farmer Hardacre!"

"Huh!" grunted the farmer.

"Cheer up!" smiled the Elf. "It could have been worse. Why, the Elf Bull might have turned into a tiger and eaten you up!"

"I suppose so!" mumbled the farmer. "Well, I'm very sorry and I wish I could give you your bull back. But all I have left is a string of sausages." The Elf laughed and his eyes twinkled.

"Just look in the bag again," he chuckled. And when Farmer Hardacre opened it up, why, there was the Elf Bull with its shiny black coat and glittering red eyes.

"Well, I'll be blowed!" said the farmer with a smile. And gently he put the bag down on the ground.

The Bull was delighted to be back with the Elf. It frisked and snorted and tapped its silver hooves on the road. Farmer Hardacre gathered up the pony's reins and started to head for home.

"Farewell, Elf-Friend!" cried the Elf after him. "I'm glad to see you've learnt your lesson."

"And much good may it do me," sighed the farmer.

And much good it *did* do him, for in the years that followed the farmer's fields produced the finest grain, and his cows produced the thickest cream for miles around.

"One good turn deserves another!" chuckled Farmer Hardacre to himself.

And it's certain that if he ever found any Elf Bulls after that, he left them well alone.

THE END

THE GOBLINS OF GRIDDLESTONE GAP

by Philip Steele

Bob Goblin and Slob Goblin were hobgoblins, and they knew everything that went on at Griddlestone Gap. Why, there had been hobgoblins in the Gap since giants lived in the forest and wolves ran free on the hills. Now, for those of you who don't know, hobgoblins are always up to one mischief or another. And at Griddlestone Gap it was no different. Their long, bony fingers lifted latches and knocked on doors, or scrabbled at windows to frighten honest people. Children would pull bedclothes over their heads and say:

> "Gribbledy, grobbledy goblins,
> Mean as mean can be!
> Gribbledy, grobbledy goblins,
> Don't say boo to me!"

This was a bit unfair, because goblins were not really *mean*, just very, very naughty.

Bob Goblin and Slob Goblin were twins, and young twins at that, for they were only 303½ years old. And over the years they had got up to all kinds of tricks. They had tied together the parson's shoelaces, so that he tripped over as he climbed into the pulpit. They had moved a scarecrow from the field and set it down by the fire in the local inn. And they had removed all the pegs so the tents collapsed at the village fête. How the villagers had gawped!

Of the two, Slob Goblin was the craftiest, and clever with it: he could write rhymes in perfect Gobbledegook and cast spells on special days of the year. Bob Goblin was the most handsome: he had the bandiest legs, the most pointed ears, and eyes which glowed like Hallowe'en lanterns.

One fine morning, Bob and Slob were sitting on a gate, sucking some eggs they had sneaked from the henhouse.

"Have you heard, Slob?" said Bob.

"Heard what, Bob?" said Slob.

"They've built a new house at the end of Griddlestone Gap."

"Oh they have, have they?" said Slob, arching his eyebrows. He began to giggle and then to cackle. "Shall we goblinize them, then?" he croaked gleefully. And with that the hobgoblins went into a huddle and whispered secretly to each other.

46

That evening, Mr Mulberry was taking the air outside his splendid new house. The thatch was trim, the timbers strong and the garden as neat and tidy as could be. "Mr Mulberry of Griddlestone Hall," he said to himself, savouring the sound of the words with pride. Then suddenly, out of the corner of his eye, he thought he saw something slip through the grass, and a window rattled behind him.

"Mrs M!" he bellowed, striding back indoors. "Did you hear something just then?"

"Not a thing, dearest!" said his wife as she came out of the dining hall. "Now come and eat your supper, or it will get cold."

Inside, the table was piled high with Mr Mulberry's favourite dishes. He eased himself into a chair, and leaned forward to sniff the yellow roses which decorated the table.

"Wa–aa–aa–haa–haa–SHOO!!!" Mr Mulberry sneezed. "Pepper!" he exclaimed when he'd recovered enough to talk. "There's pepper on those roses or I'm a cabbage!"

"Don't be ridiculous, dearest," said Mrs Mulberry with a pitying look. "You've probably got a cold coming. Now then, have a nice bowl of soup."

As she lifted the lid of the tureen, a green frog leaped out, hopped across the tablecloth and out of the window. Mr Mulberry screamed.

Their first meal at Griddlestone Hall was not a success. There was ink in the gravy boat, salt in the custard, and cod liver oil in the port. And that was not all. When he went to bed, Mr Mulberry found spiders in his nightcap, and the bedclothes turned over at both ends. All night long there was a squeaking and a creaking, a hammering and a yammering. By four in the morning, he could stand it no more.

"Hobgoblins!" he shouted. Mrs M awoke with a start.

"I *beg* your pardon?" she said.

"Hobgoblins!" repeated Mr Mulberry. "If this isn't the work of hobgoblins, my name is not Marmaduke Mulberry! And *I* am going to catch them!"

Mr Mulberry put on his slippers and he put on his dressing gown, and he crept downstairs. In the pantry he could see a candle burning. He tiptoed in very softly. There were Bob Goblin and Slob Goblin, bold as brass, sitting on a barrel of apricots.

In a trice, Mr Mulberry tipped them in and slammed the lid down on the barrel. Carrying it over his shoulder, he ran out into the garden and threw it down the well.

"And that is the end of *that*!" he said triumphantly.

But Mr Mulberry knew little of hobgoblin habits. To a goblin, a well is the most perfect little home imaginable.

"Just the place to settle down," said Bob Goblin to Slob Goblin, climbing from the barrel and sitting on a stone ledge.

"Home, sweet home!" said Slob Goblin to Bob Goblin, as he spat out an apricot stone.

So for many a long year the happy hobgoblins lived in the well at Griddlestone Hall, and they were so busy tidying up their new home that they hardly had time to play pranks. They still live there today, it is said, but now they are old and grey, and sleep away the days. But once in a while, visitors to the hall hear knocks and bangs in the wainscotting, and window panes rattle on windless nights. And the children in the village still pull bedclothes over their heads and say:

> "Gribbledy, grobbledy goblins,
> Mean as mean can be!
> Gribbledy, grobbledy goblins,
> Don't say boo to me!"

THE END

THE WORLD'S GREATEST LEPRECHAUN HUNT

by Deborah Tyler

F ar away, in a land which was known as the Emerald Isle, there was a kingdom. It was a small kingdom and it was very poor. Its farms never seemed to thrive and even its castle was shabby. The only person in the kingdom who seemed to thrive was Prince James. He was the son of King Merrow and Queen Mag, and he was very spoiled. When he did not get just what he wanted, he would let out a high pitched squeal and start throwing things. As the Court Jester had once pointed out, he was really quite nasty.

Now the kingdom of King Merrow and Queen Mag was surrounded by magic woods. Sometimes, when people passed through them, they could hear strange

laughter. And often visitors felt as if they were being
followed by many pairs of tiny eyes or heard the patter of
tiny footsteps among the leaves. If they had been quick
enough and nimble on their feet, they might have caught
a glimpse of a green velvet waistcoat or the flash of a
bushy red beard. For the magic wood was the home of
the Leprechauns who had lived on the Emerald Isle for
years and years and years.

For those of you who have never seen a Leprechaun
before, they are very small and wear three-cornered hats,
smart breeches, red shirts and green velvet
waistcoats with shiny buttons. But the
most striking thing about them is
their hair, for it is always long
and red and matches their
bushy beards perfectly.

Now Leprechauns are tricky little creatures and usually keep well out of the way of humans, which isn't always easy. For there is a legend in the Emerald Isle that if you catch a Leprechaun and look him in the eye, a crock of gold and three wishes could be yours.

At the time of our story, Prince James had come of age, but this did not stop him from throwing the most terrible tantrums! If the King asked him to do something, he usually shouted "Shan't" and pulled a face. He was sulking terribly on the day of his birthday because he wanted to have a huge birthday party and his mother and father couldn't afford it. They had spoiled him for so long, they had no money left.

"It's no good," the King said one day. "We need a crock of gold. We shall have to capture a Leprechaun! Send for my knights." So, the best knights in the kingdom were sent for and they all set out on what came to be known as "The World's Greatest Leprechaun Hunt".

Leprechauns are mischievous little men and they love practical jokes better than anything. So as soon as they heard that the knights were coming to track them down, they prepared many traps. The most tricky Leprechaun in the forest was called King Sean and he had a beautiful daughter called Mora, who was as lovely and as tiny as a china doll. Mora had often seen the knights before as they rode through the woods with the Prince. She was secretly in love with Prince James and owned a large picture of him.

"The World's Greatest Leprechaun Hunt" was not exactly a great triumph. One knight had followed a little man into a glade. He had stood behind a tree, preparing to pounce while the Leprechaun lit a clay pipe. Then, when he actually tried to grab his victim, he found that another little man had fastened him to the tree with strong twine.

Another knight had been chased home by four little men who had pelted him with hundreds of tiny shoes. As Leprechauns make shoes, they had a great supply. Other knights had vanished down holes, landing in thick mud when they got to the bottom. Twine and leaves had been made into catapults, which shot berries at them, and Leprechauns swung down on vines with cakes of mud that made a nasty mess of their armour. In fact, when the Prince walked over to see how the "Great Hunt" was progressing, he was almost trampled on by knights who were running away.

"Come back," shouted the Prince, but the knights just kept on running. Prince James leant against a tree. "It's all my fault that the kingdom is poor," he said to himself. "But what on earth can I do to put things right?" Just then he heard a tiny voice.

"Please sir," it said, "I can help you." James looked up and saw Mora standing before him. She was the smallest and prettiest girl that he had ever seen. "I can find you a Leprechaun," she said. "My father is their King." So saying, she took the Prince by the hand and led him to her father. When her father heard her step, he turned round and looked James straight in the eye. Thus it was that Prince James could claim a crock of gold and three wishes.

"Well!" said Sean crossly. "Name your first wish."

The Prince thought hard and, though he knew he should do otherwise, he decided that the kingdom could wait.

"I want a new horse," he said. There was a flash of emerald light and a lovely white horse stood before him. "I wanted a black one," said James rudely. The Leprechaun went red in the face.

"What is your second wish?" he said angrily.

"A new coat," said James, who had decided that the kingdom could wait until last. There was a flash of blue light and a brilliant sapphire coat appeared upon the Prince's back, which fastened itself up rather neatly.

"It's too tight," whined the Prince.

"NO!" said the Leprechaun King, bristling with rage. "You are too FAT! I am tired of your moanin' and groanin' and will not grant your last wish until you take me to the palace." Then he jumped upon the horse and got Mora

57

and James to do the same.

They rode to the court and when they got there, King Sean told Mag and Merrow the whole story. The King and Queen were ashamed of their son's behaviour and were sorry that he was so spoiled. In short, they wished to teach him a lesson, but they didn't know how.

"I will give you one last wish and the crock of gold if I can have a wish of my own granted," said the little man. The King and Queen agreed and their son sulked.

So, under much protest, the Prince asked for a prosperous kingdom. When he had done so, all the castle shook and there was a blinding ray of pink light before their eyes. When it had gone, the castle gleamed as if it had been painted, the grass glowed a rich, emerald green, and the flowers in all the window boxes blossomed like jewels. On all the farms, the cattle grew fat and crops grew tall.

"Now for my wish," said the little man. "I want your son to marry my daughter, as she loves him – although I wish I knew why." The royal couple agreed at once for they thought Mora was lovely, and the Prince, well, he just sulked.

The wedding date was set without the consent of the Prince. The castle chapel was decorated with glittering paper shamrocks, pale green candles, and berries and wild roses from the forest. On the day of the wedding, Mora wore a lovely gown of woven water lilies and spiders' webs. The Prince was so cross about the whole affair that he had gone purple in the face, which really matched his robes very well. The ceremony was about to begin, and knights and Leprechauns filled the pews, when Mora cried,

"Stop!" The whole court was silent. "I cannot marry you, unless you love me for myself," she continued. "Your selfishness has made everyone unhappy, even you. Now it is time you started behaving like a proper prince." Suddenly James realised how dreadful he had been. He thought of his poor father and mother and how awful

he had been to everyone. Above all, he saw how horrid he had been to Mora, who had loved him so unselfishly, when really he had secretly loved her all along!

"I will marry you Mora," said James, "and I will be a well-loved prince!" Mora smiled and so the wedding ceremony began. And when James finally kissed his bride, she grew to be as tall as he was. King Sean went back to his home in the magic woods, though he always went to the castle for tea on Sundays, and the Leprechauns carried on playing tricks on anyone who went looking for crocks of gold behind the trees. Even today, if you should ever travel to the Emerald Isle and walk through the woods there, you just might be lucky enough to hear Leprechaun laughter from among the trees or catch a climpse of a bushy red beard, or a velvet waistcoat fastened with shiny buttons.

THE END